PRINCESS POSEY

and the

PERFECT PRESENT

Stephanie Greene

ILLUSTRATED BY
Stephanie Roth Sisson

PUFFIN BOOKS
An Imprint of Penguin Group (USA)

PUFFIN BOOKS
Published by the Penguin Group
Penguin Group (USA) LLC
375 Hudson Street
New York, New York 10014

USA * Canada * UK * Ireland * Australia
New Zealand * India * South Africa * China

penguin.com
A Penguin Random House Company

Published simultaneously in the United States of America by G. P. Putnam's Sons
and Puffin Books, divisions of Penguin Young Readers Group, 2011

THE LIBRARY OF CONGRESS HAS CATALOGED THE G. P. PUTNAM'S SONS EDITION AS FOLLOWS:
Greene, Stephanie.
Princess Posey and the perfect present / Stephanie Greene ;
illustrated by Stephanie Roth Sisson.
p. cm.
Summary: For first-grader Posey, every school day is great until her teacher's
birthday, when her best friend's gift of an enormous bouquet puts
Posey's few, home-grown roses to shame.
ISBN: 978-0-399-25462-8 (hardcover)
[1. Teachers—Fiction. 2. Schools—Fiction. 3. Best friends—Fiction.
4. Friendship—Fiction.]
I. Sisson, Stephanie Roth, ill. II. Title
PZ7.G8434Pri 2011
[Fic]—dc22 2010001276

Puffin Books ISBN 978-0-14-241828-4

Printed in the United States of America

9 10

CONTENTS

HAPPY WALKING

"Remember when I was afraid to walk into school by myself?" said Posey. "I was silly, wasn't I, Mom?"

Her mom stopped the car in front of the school.

"You weren't silly," she said. "You were just out of kindergarten."

The girls in Posey's class said the word *silly* all the time. Sometimes it meant "funny." Other times it meant "babyish."

"I bet Danny will be afraid to walk into school by himself, won't he?" said Posey.

Her baby brother kicked his feet against his car seat and reached out his hand.

Posey shook it.

"Danny's lucky," her mom said.

"He has a big sister to show him how."

Posey got out of the car and shut the door. "See you later, alligator," she called.

"After a while, crocodile," her mom called back.

Posey walked into the school and down to the blue hall. Miss Lee was standing outside their classroom door.

"Miss Lee!" Posey called. "Hi, Miss Lee!"

She knew children were supposed to walk in the halls at Middle Pond School.

Not run.

But Posey couldn't help it. When she saw her very own teacher

5

standing outside their door, she started to skip.

She was careful to skip her tiny inside skip. Not her big outside skip. Besides, skipping wasn't running. It was happy walking.

And Posey was happy.

She loved her big classroom where she could see all her friends.

She loved having her own cubby with her name over it.

She loved raising her hand when she knew the answer to a question. And she loved her two best friends, Ava and Nikki.

But most of all, Posey loved her teacher, Miss Lee.

CHAPTER TWO

ANOTHER GREAT DAY

"**G**ood morning, Posey," Miss Lee said. "You're very cheerful this morning."

"See my new kitty eraser?" said Posey.

"It's very nice," said Miss Lee. "Make sure you keep it in your cubby."

"I will." Posey pulled a piece of paper out of her backpack. "Look what I made for you."

"Another drawing?" Miss Lee shook her head. "I don't know how you find time to sleep."

Posey laughed. She loved it when Miss Lee teased her.

"It's a pink rainbow!" Miss Lee sounded amazed.

"I used three different pinks," Posey said.

"I see that." Miss Lee smiled. "I have never seen a rainbow like this before."

"It's the only one in the world," said Posey.

"In that case, I think we need to hang it in our gallery, don't you?" said Miss Lee.

"Oh, yes!"

That was exactly what Posey had hoped Miss Lee was going to

The Learners' Gallery

say. The Learners' Gallery was where they hung special stories and drawings.

Their class was called "Miss Lee's Learners."

Learning was very important work.

In first grade they learned new things all day long.

How to spell new words. How to write stories. How to add numbers like two plus three.

Posey was proud to be one of Miss Lee's Learners. She was excited to have her drawing hang in the Learners' Gallery, too.

"There. How's that?" Miss Lee stood back to admire Posey's picture.

"Beautiful," said Posey.

She went to her cubby and put away her things. She looked around for Ava and Nikki. There they were, in front of the word wall! Posey saw Ava's blond curls and Nikki's black ones.

"Hi, Ava! Hi, Nikki!" Posey skipped over to them. "How do you like my new kitty eraser?"

"I wish I had one," said Nikki.

"Maybe you can try mine tomorrow," said Posey.

"Can I try it, too?" Ava asked.

"Okay."

The three friends hugged.

It was going to be another great day in first grade.

CHAPTER THREE

"WHOOSH!"

Gramps picked up Posey after school. There was a bag of mulch in the back of his truck.

"I bet today is gardening day," Posey said.

"How did you get to be so smart?" said Gramps. "I promised your mom I would get her flower beds ready for winter."

"Can I help?" asked Posey.

"I'm counting on it," Gramps said.

After Posey had her snack, she went to her room to put on her pink tutu. It was her favorite thing to wear.

She never told anyone, but when she wore her pink tutu, she was Princess Posey, the Pink Princess.

Princess Posey could go anywhere and do anything.

Especially if she had her magic princess wand. Posey picked it up.

She had made it herself with a stick and tinfoil.

It had a star at the end, too.

Posey waved it in the air as she ran outside. She was going to use it now to help the flowers grow.

The yellow flowers were first.

"Whoosh!" Princess Posey made her magic wand noise and waved it over the flowers. "I hereby command you to grow!" she said.

"Whoosh!" Posey commanded the blue flowers.

"Whoosh!" she told the white flowers.

The pink roses were last. They were her favorite. She had helped Gramps plant them.

"You are the most beautifulest flowers in the whole garden," she said.

"Whoosh!"

"Hey!" Gramps called. He was kneeling on the grass beside a pile of mulch. "Where's my best helper?"

Posey ran over to him. "I was playing a game," she said.

"I figured as much." Gramps held out his hand. "I wanted you to see this before it flew away."

A ladybug with four black dots was crawling in the palm of Gramps's hand.

"It means good luck, doesn't it?" said Posey.

"Sure does," said Gramps.

"Ladybug,
ladybug, fly
away home,"
Posey said.

Just like that,
the ladybug opened
its wings and lifted into the air.

"I guess you told it a thing or
two," said Gramps. "Dig in."

Posey scooped up two handfuls
of mulch. "I'll make sure the roses
are warm," she said.

"That's my girl," Gramps said.
"They will thank you for it, too."

CHAPTER
FOUR

MISS LEE'S NEWS

At the end of school the next day, Miss Lee called, "Boys and girls. I have a special announcement."

A special announcement! Posey put down her pencil. Everyone around her did, too.

"Guess what tomorrow is?" Miss Lee asked.

"Wednesday!" Luca shouted.

Posey frowned. That Luca! He always forgot to raise his hand. Miss Lee usually reminded him. All she did now was smile.

"That's right, Luca. It's Wednesday," she said. "But it's also my birthday."

Miss Lee's birthday! How exciting!

"It's my turn to bring in birthday cupcakes," Miss Lee said. "We'll celebrate after lunch."

Everyone started to talk. The room buzzed like the inside of a beehive. Posey got in line with Ava and Nikki to wait for the bell.

"I'm going to bring Miss Lee a present," Nikki said.

"Me too," said Ava. "I'm going to bring her something very special!"

"I'm going to bring her something very, very special!" said Nikki. "How about you, Posey?"

Posey knew exactly what she was going to bring. Her present was going to be very, very, *very* special.

THE VERY, VERY, VERY SPECIAL PRESENT

"Hurry, Danny, hurry!" Posey cried. She ran across the backyard.

"He's coming as fast as he can," her mom said. She held Danny's hand to keep him from falling.

Danny couldn't walk by himself yet. All he did was stumble and fall, stumble and fall.

Every time he fell on his bottom, he laughed. Most of the time Posey laughed with him.

Today she wanted him to go faster.

"See, Mom?" Posey said. She waited for them in front of the roses. "One, two, three, four, five! Miss Lee will love them, won't she?"

"I'm sure she will," said her mom.

"Let's leave this one." Posey
pointed to a tiny bud. It was still
closed. "It hasn't been born yet."

"Maybe we should cut them in
the morning," said her mom.

"Danny might spill his cereal

in the morning," said Posey. "We
might be late."

"Okay."

Her mom cut the roses. Posey
carried them inside. She wrapped
the stems in a wet paper towel.

Then she wrapped foil around the paper towel and put the roses in the refrigerator.

"I bet no one else gives Miss Lee such a special present," she said. "She'll be amazed, won't she, Mom?"

"She'll love them because you grew them," said her mom.

Posey could hardly wait to see Miss Lee's face. She was going to smile and smile.

She would know Posey liked her more than anyone.

In her secret heart, Posey hoped Miss Lee would like her more than anyone, too.

A NOT-SO-WONDERFUL SURPRISE

Posey held her roses tight as she walked slowly down the blue hall. She didn't skip even her tiny inside skip.

Excitement butterflies were tickling the inside of her stomach.

Miss Lee was going to be so happy. She was going to say, "Why, Posey! These are the most beautiful flowers I ever saw!"

But that's not what Miss Lee said.

When Posey got to the door of their classroom, she heard Miss Lee say, "Why, Nikki! What beautiful flowers!"

Oh, no!

Posey stopped.

Miss Lee and Nikki were standing by Miss Lee's desk. Miss Lee was holding the biggest bunch of flowers Posey had ever seen.

They were every color. They were wrapped in beautiful green paper.

The paper was tied with glittery ribbons that curled at the ends.

"We got them in a store that had nothing but flowers," Nikki said.

"It's called a florist," said Miss Lee. "We'll put that word on the word wall today."

She smiled at Nikki. Nikki smiled back.

Posey's heart felt like it was being squeezed.

"I have just the thing for them!"

Miss Lee said. She went to her closet and took out a vase. "How would you like to fill it with water for me?"

"Sure!" said Nikki.

Nikki filled Miss Lee's "just the thing!" vase with water. After Miss Lee put in the flowers, she wound the glittery ribbons around her wrist like a bracelet.

She and Nikki laughed.

Posey's mouth felt trembly. Her eyes felt hot. Quiet as a mouse, she went back into the hall.

Nikki's flowers were so beautiful!
Posey couldn't give five little roses
that were wrapped in a soggy paper
towel to Miss Lee now.

Yesterday they looked so beautiful. Today they looked so small.

The tinfoil was crumpled where Posey had gripped it. One of the roses had a droopy head like it was sleepy.

Looking at them made Posey feel sad.

She put them in her backpack. She zipped it closed.

Now Miss Lee wouldn't know how much Posey liked her.

Now she would like Nikki more than she liked Posey.

CHAPTER
SEVEN

"YOU'RE NOT MY FRIEND"

Ava and Nikki rushed up to Posey's table.

"Miss Lee loved the story I wrote for her!" Ava said.

"She loved my flowers, too!" said Nikki. "What did you give her, Posey?"

"I don't like you anymore,
Nikki," Posey said with her trembly
mouth. "You're not my friend."

Nikki's eyes got big the way they did when she was going to cry.

Posey turned around in her chair so she couldn't see. Being mean made her feel a little better.

But not for long.

She didn't have anyone to share her cookies with at lunch. She sat by herself on the swings at recess.

When Miss Lee asked for helpers to pass out her birthday cupcakes, Posey didn't raise her hand.

The cupcakes had fluffy white frosting. They were covered with colored sprinkles.

Posey didn't touch hers.

Miss Lee walked around the room. She stopped at every table.

"Aren't you going to eat yours?" she said when she got to Posey.

Posey shook her head.

"You have been quiet all day," said Miss Lee. "Do you feel all right?"

Posey nodded.

Miss Lee crouched down. "Would you like to talk about it?" she whispered.

Posey shook her head again. This time, she squeezed her eyes shut.

"All right." Miss Lee stood up.

"I'll wrap this so you can take it home."

Posey watched Miss Lee walk away. She *did* want to talk about it. But not with Miss Lee.

With her mom.

Except, when Posey opened the car door after school and her mom said, "How did Miss Lee like your roses?" Posey didn't talk.

She cried.

CHAPTER EIGHT

AS GOOD AS NEW

"There." Posey's mom put the last rose into the jar of water. She had snipped off the tips of each stem so they could drink.

"They will be as good as new in no time," she said.

Posey sniffed. She had told her mom what happened. Except not the part where she was mean to Nikki.

"Can Danny have a piece of your cupcake?" her mom said.

"I guess so."

Her mom put a piece of cupcake on the tray of Danny's high chair. She sat down at the kitchen table next to Posey.

"I'm sorry you were disappointed, Posey," she said. "But you should have given Miss Lee your flowers."

"Nikki's not my friend anymore," Posey said.

"You're being silly." Her mom tucked a piece of hair behind Posey's ear. "Nikki didn't know you were bringing flowers, did she?"

"No."

Posey had kept her idea a secret, but Nikki came up with it, too. They came up with the same good idea lots of times. That's why they were best friends.

She had hurt the feelings of one of her own best friends.

Posey's mouth got trembly again.

"But she gave Miss Lee about fifty hundred," she said.

"The number doesn't matter," her mom said. "Look at Danny!

We only have one of him and that's plenty, don't you think?"

When Posey and her mom looked at him, Danny laughed.

He had frosting all over his face. One blue sprinkle sat on the tip of his nose. He was spreading more frosting on the tray of his high chair.

"If we had more than one Danny, the house would be a mess!" Posey said.

"Exactly." Her mom laughed as she stood up. "You go get changed while I clean him up," she said. "We'll play outside for a bit."

"But how will Miss Lee know I like her?" Posey said.

"You'll find a way to show her," her mom said. "Your very own Posey way."

CHAPTER NINE

SILLY POSEY!

Posey put on her pink tutu. She also put on her pink veil. It always made her feel better.

Gramps gave it to her for the first day of first grade. It was covered with stars.

Posey went outside. The sun was warm on her face. She closed her eyes and held out her arms.

She was Princess Posey.

Princess Posey was lying on a soft pink cloud. The cloud was slowly drifting across the sky. A striped pink rainbow curved high above her head.

The stars on her veil sparkled in the sun.

Princess Posey was beautiful and kind. She wouldn't cry if someone gave the same present. She would just think of another present.

An even more special present.

Of course!

Posey opened her eyes. She stamped her foot.

You're a *silly* Posey, she told herself.

All she had to do was think of another present.

An after-birthday present! That was it! Miss Lee probably never got an after-birthday present before.

What could she bring? Where could it be?

Posey suddenly saw it.

The tiny rose that was left on the bush had opened in the night.

Today was the rose's birthday, too!

Posey crept close and saw the most amazing thing. A ladybug had crawled inside. It was nestled between the petals, fast asleep.

"Ladybug, ladybug, don't fly away home," Posey whispered. "I'm taking you to school tomorrow."

JUST THE THING
FOR IT!

Posey tiptoed down the hall to her classroom. She didn't make a peep. The ladybug stayed fast asleep.

"Hi, Miss Lee," she said.

Miss Lee spun around. "Oh, Posey!" she said. "You were so quiet that I didn't hear you come in."

79

"I brought you an after-birthday present," said Posey. She held out the rose. "Yesterday was its birthday, too."

"I've never gotten an after-birthday present before," Miss Lee said. "It's beautiful."

"It will bring you good luck," said Posey.

"It will?"

"Look." Posey pointed at the ladybug.

"Oh, my." Miss Lee sounded amazed. "I think it might be the

only lucky, after-birthday rose in the world, don't you?"

"It is," said Posey.

"I have just the thing for it!" Miss Lee went to her closet and took out a small thin vase. "It's called a bud vase," she said. "It only holds one flower."

"Two would be crowded," said Posey.

"Exactly." Miss Lee smiled. "Would you like to fill it with water for me?"

"Okay."

Posey filled the vase with water. Miss Lee put in the rose.

It was a perfect fit.

"I feel lucky already to have

a girl as thoughtful as you in my class, Posey," Miss Lee said. "Thank you."

"You're welcome."

Posey went to her cubby and put away her pack. Ava and Nikki were sitting on the floor in the reading corner.

"Can I play?" Posey said.

"You were mean to me," Nikki told her.

"I'm sorry. I was being silly." Posey sat down next to her. "You can use my kitty eraser today."

"Okay," said Nikki.

"Can I use it, too?" asked Ava.

"You can share it," Posey told her.

"We're playing family," Nikki said. "We're both mothers and our babies are asleep."

"I'll be the baby that woke up," Posey said. "Wah-wah!" She crawled onto Nikki and Ava's laps.

"Oh, Posey, you're so silly," Nikki said.

"Wah-wah," said Posey. "Me have wet diaper."

"Posey!" Ava cried.

Nikki and Posey giggled.

It was going to be another great day in first grade.

❀ ❀ ❀

P✿SEY'S PAGES

Make your own magic
princess wand! All you need
is aluminum foil, a piece of
cardboard, a pair of scissors,
and a stick about the size
of a pencil.

1. Tear off a piece of foil that's three
inches wide. Wrap it around your stick.

2. Draw a star on the piece of
cardboard and cut it out.

3. Tear off a large piece of foil. Cut it into strips that are about a half inch wide.

4. Put the top of your stick in the middle of the star. Wrap the foil strips around the points of the star and then around the stick until the star is secure.

5. Wrap your star in another piece of foil to cover all of the strips.

Decorate your wand with sparkly glue, stickers, or ribbons, if you want. My wand goes WHOOSH! What sound does yours make?

Watch for the next **PRINCESS POSEY** book!

PRINCESS POSEY
and the
NEXT-DOOR
DOG

When Posey was little, a dog jumped on her in the park and knocked her down. She still remembers the scary feeling. But can she get over it to help a dog in trouble?